T0196967

THE HAND

J. L. Simmons

Illustrations by **Kenn Yapsangco**

Order this book online at www.trafford.com
or email orders@trafford.com

Most Trafford titles are also available at major online book retailers.

Boy Scouts Handbook, New Brunswick, NJ U.S.A.: Boy Scouts of America seventh edition third printing Page 31, 1967. [1]
Crystal Vurroughs – Story Sequence Editing
Dee Reston / Kenn Yapsangco - Illustrations
Gary Dangel – Photo Editing
Joe Simmons Jr. – Scene Staging, Beta Reader
Marie Giles – Editing
Olivia Orso – Scene Staging
Elizabeth Simmons –Story Critique, Beta Reader
Janee Simmons - Beta Reader
Lovieree Simmons – Beta Reader

Thanks to friends at Hueston Woods State Park for the great pictures

Printed in the United States of America.

ISBN: 978-1-4907-4220-5 (sc)
978-1-4907-4219-9 (e)

Library of Congress Control Number: 2014912974

Trafford rev. 09/26/2014

www.trafford.com
North America & international
toll-free: 1 888 232 4444 (USA & Canada)
fax: 812 355 4082

Driving up Oxford College Corner Road (Highway 27), I turned on the right signal. "We are almost to the campsite now, to start the families' annual camping trip, marking the end of another school year. We are about two miles away." I turned right onto Todd Road. The noise level rose in the van, with all the passengers yelling with excitement. Driving down Todd Road, on the left there was a sign coming up, Wood for Sale.

Firewood
for
Sale

“Dad, are we going to get wood now? It’ll be more expensive at the camp store,” said Reena.

You have a point, I thought. Slowing down, I turned on the left signal, a slow roll off the street into the driveway. *Good, there is a man by the piles of wood.*

The van doors opened; my children and their friends fell out. After grabbing a few dollars from the envelope in the cup holder, I stepped out of the van. Immediately I saw a familiar face from the past. *How do I know this guy, sitting by the entrance of a yard with piles of wood*? I too must have looked familiar to him since his long, unblinking gaze was also on me. We made eye contact, and immediately I blurted out, “Ranger Washington!”

“Did you work at Houston Woods in security back in early ’90s?” Immediately he recalled my face as we both went back to a terrifying weekend in May of 1992. I remembered vividly the night his face became disfigured.

He smiled from a scarred face and said, “No, I am not a ranger.”

The children respectfully waited quietly to find out to whom I was talking.

With soft smiles, we exchanged pleasantries. “It has been a minute,” I said.

“Yes, it has been a few years since the last time we spoke,” Mr. Washington said. “How is your wife doing?”

The children wondered how he knew their mother. “She is doing well. We have three children now.” I introduced each from oldest to youngest. “My daughter Reena; son, LJ; and youngest daughter, Naya.”

“The missus is not with y’all?” Mr. Washington asked.

“No, she does not enjoy camping and has not been camping for years.” Actually, she had not been camping since the last time he saw her. “How about you? How are you doing? Are you married?”

“The missus and I have one child. She is in college, in the army’s ROTC program. My lawn care business is keeping the lights on.”

“It is good seeing you. I pass this way whenever I go camping. In the future, I will blow the car horn if I see you sitting out.”

“You do that.”

“Do you have any hardwood? I need a few pieces of soft—and hardwood for a campfire tonight. We got off to a very late start due to a parent having last-minute car troubles and some campers getting dropped off later than expected. We will not have time to cook anything over the fire tonight. We just left the superstore a few miles back to pick up dinner for tonight.”

“Yes, I have the wood you need, but where are you going to put them? Surely not on top of the pizza. Your van is full,” Mr. Washington asked, looking amused.

We laughed. “Each person will have to hold a piece of wood, and a log or two will need to be put on the floor behind their feet . . . Are you still working at Houston Woods?”

“No, I quit a few years after the hand incident.”

After Mr. Washington helped to strategically place the wood into the van and I paid him, we prepared to part ways. Mr. Washington handed me one more piece of oak wood through my window for me to hold on my lap. “Thanks, Mr. Washington.”

“Please, call me Keef.”

“Well again, thanks, Keef, for the wood. Have a great day.”

“You too. Give my best to your wife.”

“Likewise.”

Keef waved us off. “Make sure you keep a strong fire going, and keep your tents zipped from the floor to the roof!” he reminded.

“Will do!” I replied.

The sun was about to touch the treetops; we really needed to get to our campsite and start putting up tents.

I backed the van up and prepared to pull away, then asked, “What time will you be out tomorrow, in case we need to buy more wood and maybe we can get caught up?”

Keef said, “Around the same time, around sunset. If I am not sitting out here, just blow the horn.” A look passed between us—we both knew that I would be returning alone tomorrow.

A half mile down the road, as I turned right onto Jones/Butler Israel Road, questions came from all directions: “What is the hand incident?”

“What did he mean, ‘Make sure you keep a strong fire going’?”

“Yeah, what did he mean, ‘Keep your tents zipped from the floor to the roof’?”

“Why hasn’t Mom been camping since 1992?”

To delay further questions, I said, “Y’all quiet down. We’re getting ready to make a sharp turn down to the main loop. I need to focus.” Once the turn was completed, the questions were asked again. “We have arrived.”

Some first-timers started reading the signs. “There is a beach here?” one asked as we passed sailboats on the right.

We could see Acton Lake ahead. The street ended, and I made a left turn then drove over a stream, passing basketball courts and cookout areas.

The kids started to spout out the variety of things to do: “There is a hotel here!”

“There is a nature center here?”

"I want to go horseback riding."

"Will we go to the Indian mound?"

"This place must be huge."

"They have cabins here. Are we staying in cabins?"

Everyone yelled, "No!" Not after all the tents we packed! Excitement started to build with the many different things each would get to do this weekend.

PRIMITIVE CAMP SITES
NON - PRIMITIVE CAMP SITES

At the second stream, folks were putting up their fishing poles because it was getting late. I turned left toward the camp store. In a few minutes, we were on our way. At the fork in the road, one arrowed sign pointed right to primitive camping and the other arrowed sign pointed left to non-primitive camping. We proceeded to the left.

"What is the difference between the primitive and non-primitive campsites?" asked an excited camper.

I smiled. "The big difference is the non-primitive have showers, toilets, running water, and electric."

The natural next questions followed: "Where do the primitive campers use the bathroom? How do they wash their hands?"

"I don't know," I said. "It is getting dark fast. Let's get the campsite set up quickly. We can talk about your questions around the campfire." We unloaded the van, started setup. I assigned each teen a task.

When I thought all was going well, Naya asked, "Who is Mr. Washington?"

"For now, I will say Mr. Keef was in charge of security the first time your mother and I camped at Houston Woods." I answered, "We need to keep it moving and finish setting up the camp."

We had to use the van's headlights to finish getting the girls' tent set up. I managed to get the food tent set up and a fire going while the boys were setting up our tent. The tents were all up but not tied down properly. Debris was hanging out the tents and lying around on the ground. We would tidy up in the morning; everyone was tired by now.

Most were sitting around the campfire, some were in the food tent getting a drink or eating pizza from a local restaurant, while others returned from the shower house toilets. The fire felt nice as the evening began to cool down. The cracking and popping sounds of the burning wood were soothing. We could hear the campground quiet down; we began to hear nearby fires along with the sounds of voices and animals. The lack of a breeze allowed the smoke to rise straight up. Even my children and their friends spoke in soft tones to not disturb the night or our neighbors.

"I am so tired, but I do not want to leave the warm fire," some commented.

Another started talking about the first thing they were going to do the next morning.

One was going Putt-Putting; another was going to the beach.

Then a few chimed in, "I am going with you!"

"Dad, what is the hand incident?" asked Naya, driving a pause in the conversation.

"Baby girl, many years have passed. My details may be a little fuzzy. This is some of your friends' first time camping. I do not want to disturb them."

Their friends seemed confident they would not be bothered. "Go ahead, Mr. Simpson, it is okay—we'll be fine."

I went around to each child and asked them individually; they all said they would be okay. While they were answering, I put another log of oak and a log of pine into the fire.

"Okay, where should I start?"

"Wait, wait a minute!" The girls grabbed a blanket out of their tent and put it across their shoulders and backs. The boys pulled their arms inside their shirts. A few minutes later, everyone said, "Go ahead, we're ready now!" The girls giggled. The boys sighed.

"Again, where should I start? Keep in mind the hand incident is disturbing for me as well. There may be things too troubling for me to talk about."

The unsympathetic voices of my children said, "Go ahead, Dad!"

"You already know the last time your mother went camping was in May 1992. That was when your mother and I met Mr. Keef, the first and last time before today. He was Ranger Washington then. To answer a question from earlier, 'Why does Mom not go camping?' I think the hand incident is the key reason that she does not go camping. She was there when Ranger Washington and I relived the events of the evening and compared notes from each other's perspective.

"For her, the hand incident starts with caution. But can be experienced through the sounds in the night, the feeling that moves through the woods as the sun sets and trees begin to fall asleep, the sightings imagined that some contribute to the trickery of the campfire light. Ultimately, the experience culminates with taking precaution. Your mother does not like the fact that so many tears could have been saved if precaution was practiced.

"Even now, I get goose bumps the closer the hour gets to midnight and the campground prepares to transition from today into tomorrow."

"What is the hand incident?" LJ asked impatiently.

"Saturday, May 9, 1992, my friends Ty, Tee, your mother, and I were camping for the weekend. Actually, the next row over, Row C. It was a cool night in mid spring. It was cooler than tonight, and there was almost a full moon. The campsites were not full. Ranger Washington was slowly rolling through the campsites. He stopped and talked to most of us that night. He gave us an update on all who were on the grounds.

"He said, 'Hello. Where did you folk come from?'

"'We came from Cincinnati.'

"'We have another group up from Cincinnati, a good-size group.'

"We had noticed that campers were sparse that night. There were probably seven campsites being used that evening, including the large group of eighteen up from Cincinnati, Ohio. There were even fewer campers in the primitive sites. I think Ranger Washington said there was only one site being used in the primitive area that night, two friends sharing a campsite.

"We continued with pleasantries a few minutes more. Ranger Washington said, 'The air feels different tonight,' then rolled away to chat with the next campers on our row and repeated the conversation.

"It was an evening that none of us would ever forget! The air really did feel different, cooler and crisper. Sounds were—how can I describe the clarity in the air? Let's just say I could hear my own heartbeat that night. Oh yes, on that night, the campfire sounds stood out in my mind. The popping of the hot embers as they fell from the burning wood sounded loud like small-caliber gunfire. All seemed okay, too perfect if you ask. Yes, too perfect.

"As time passed, 9:45, 10:50 p.m., I could not then and cannot today say what was different, what changed as the night moved on, but something was different, definitely different. Ranger Washington was not the only one to sense something unusual. As he drove through the RV section of the campground near the path to the Indian mound, an RV camper waved him to stop. Ranger Washington pulled over to chat briefly. As he drove onto their campsite area, other RV campers came out to meet his car.

"A camper said, 'Hello.' Ranger Washington asked, 'Is it quiet enough for you?'

"They chuckled.

"The camper said, 'Yes, my dog, Biscuit, is acting strange. This breeze is a little too much for me. The air is chilling me to the bone.' They chuckled again. The breeze was so slight the leaves were not moving.

"A camper said, 'My wife said it feels like death is in the air. She said the night's calm was reminding her of the night their pet cat died a few weeks prior.' The wife said that she was starting to get goose bumps and felt like a weight was on her chest.

"Ranger Washington asked if he needed to call an ambulance. The wife said no and went inside the RV.

"After an uneasy chuckle, the camper said that he had heard a noise in the bushes. He pointed to a patch of woods between a swing set and a small shed. Biscuit started barking.

Ranger Washington flashed his flashlight in the direction of the woods and saw two white eyes looking back. The eyes were frozen, not moving. Biscuit barked and chased the animal away. 'Damn raccoons, spooked my wife,' said the camper. They both laughed.

"Ranger Washington told the camper, 'Between us, it scared me too!'

"To reassure the campers that all was well, Ranger Washington told them he had worked at the park for years. 'We have not had any problems here.'

"He was surprised though that so few people were out camping after consecutive days of warm weather. 'It looks like the weather reports has scared away folk again.' It was supposed to rain the previous day, that day, and the next day. 'But this campsite has not seen one drop of rain!' They laughed about the weather scaring away campers. 'Good night!' said Ranger Washington, as he needed to finish making the rounds. Ranger Washington asked the camper to give his best to the missus and rolled away.

"Ranger Washington understood what the camper's wife was feeling—the more he drove around the campgrounds, the more uneasy he became. Ranger Washington wondered what was going on. He had his Bible on the seat and moved it to the dashboard and kept making his rounds. Ranger Washington shined his light into the woods periodically and saw white eyes gazing back at him. The raccoons were all over the place.

“Ranger Washington recalled the two friends sharing a campsite in the primitive section. They were in a site near the entrance of the primitive section, immediately off the little Four Mile Creek.

“No one is sure what happened, but according to the federal reconstruction specialist, ‘While sitting around the campfire, enjoying a few alcoholic beverages, their temperament changed along with the mood of the woods. They began to argue about minor things like the best sports player, engine block modifications, and who caught the largest crappie. The more they drank, the more they fought with words, and soon things escalated to fists, then to pocket knife, and then hatchet.’

“Ranger Washington said he had heard the commotion as he drove around the camp store, put a call in for backup, and spun his tires to start driving toward the primitive section with his car windows mostly raised and the heat on inside the car. The chill in the air was unreal. As he entered the entrance of the primitive section, Ranger Washington heard the yells. The noise stopped suddenly. He observed the wind that once swept through the treetops stopped and was replaced with a slow, bone-chilling breeze that seemed to move through the campground. Even with the car heat on, the chill moved through him, his hair stood up on his arms and the back of his neck.

“Off in the distance, it sounded like in the direction of the camp store, at the bottom of the hill, I heard spinning tires like someone was in a big hurry. Others in the RV camping area *started walking through the woods in the direction of the commotion. I did not know the woods that well, so I asked your mother to stay with Ty and Tee. I jumped on a bike and rode down the hill toward the camp store. En route I could hear off in the distance the sounds of multiple types of sirens. I turned left at the bottom of the hill into the direction of the primitive campsite area.*

“Something else was odd that evening, Ranger Washington recalled in his thoughts to me later. ‘As the chilling breeze moved through the campground, thoughts of spirits and demons crossed my mind, and during those moments, the only sounds I heard were the cracking and thrashing noises. Raccoons, skunks, and opossums were scurrying in front of and behind my car. I heard muffled sounds through the partially raised windows. It sounded like someone lying on the leaves and sticks, kicking their legs, and hitting the ground with their fist. I heard no words from the friends, just the struggling, more thrashing, a soft thud, and then no more movement.’

“Panic began to set in. Ranger Washington said, ‘As I got closer to the campsite of the friends, it seemed like my eyes might have been playing tricks on me. I swore that behind the fire well, I could barely make out what looked like a body lying face up with his left forearm on the rim of the fire well while his hand cooked over the fire. On the back side of the fire, in front of the fire well, I could see the other friend more clearly, he was moving strangely. It seemed like he was being slowly jerked and dragged—by what, I could not make out. The closer my car got to the campsite, the more cautious I became. I called dispatch again to report two men down. I saw the right arm of the body in front of the fire move up and down slowly, it barely reached the edge of the fire well as it squirted and oozed blood. Where is the hand? Is it in the fire? I wondered if this was a trick. Now, it looked like someone was moving the body with strings, as one would control a puppet.’

POLICE
POLICE
LJJ-07E

"In disbelief, Ranger Washington thought to himself, 'What the! Is that a tarantula? No, it looks more like a hand, yes, a hand.' Ranger Washington said that he was not sure what he was watching. 'I watched the hand figure flatten itself, crawl under the right elbow, and raise itself to the fingertips, forcing the severed arm to move up beyond the rim of the fire well and allow more blood to ooze.' The arm gave barely a squirt of blood. Ranger Washington recalled rolling down his window and yelling 'Git!' No one moved! He blew the car horn. The handlike object ignored him and slowly moved from under the elbow to under the neck and chin. Then the head moved forward, but the body did not move. 'It was very strange to see. The hand kept maneuvering the head,' Ranger Washington said. He thought the neck would stretch to the point of separating the head from the body. Eventually, the body got dragged forward an inch or more. Again Ranger Washington yelled 'Git!' and flashed his spotlight onto the body. 'Git, git out of here!' Again nothing and no one moved!

"Ranger Washington stepped out of the car to use his binoculars. Still he could not see movement from either man. He walked around behind the car to the passenger side, using the door as a shield. Ranger Washington stood in the space between the car door and the body of the car. With his left foot raised to the toes, he craned to see more with the binoculars, but still he could not see anything. One last time, Ranger Washington stepped down and rested both elbows on the roof of the car to study the campsite to get and pass more information to the fast-approaching law enforcement and ambulances. Still he could not see anything.

"Ranger Washington said he gathered his nerves, called again for backup. Then he grabbed his flashlight and baton and added some bass to his throat to hide his fear as he again yelled 'Git!' and 'Are y'all okay?' Nothing! No response. The body continued to move closer to the fire well. 'Git!' Ranger Washington was starting to sound like a scared child with his flashlight held high in his right hand and baton in the left.

"Ranger Washington's underarms became wet, sweat dripped from his forehead and ran down his back. All his senses were heightened. He was too afraid to cry, too nervous to yell, too curious to turn back. Ranger Washington had to see for himself. What kind of animal was this? 'Git!' Nothing! Still, he could see slow movement under the body. Twenty steps away, he could smell burning flesh and see the camp area fully. He called out, 'Are you able to move?' Fifteen steps away, the second body stopped moving. Ranger Washington kept his flashlight shining on the second body while stepping to the left of the fire, avoiding stepping in front of his car's spotlight.

> *"At this time, only the light of the moon illuminated my ride down the dark street that separated the dense animal-populated woods on both sides. The animals were fleeing the area—snakes, deer, and raccoons kept crossing the street in front and behind me. I was so scared but could not stop pedaling. I could hear a car horn blow and few minutes later Ranger Washington's repeated yells for help. I kept going, pedaling forward. The sounds of sirens were coming closer.*

"Ranger Washington said he saw a fresh-cut, blood-stained hand crawl from under the neck, behind the body. Trailing behind the hand was part of a raw bone dragging the ground. The bone was cut above the wrist. Some of the top flesh had a clean-cut mark while the bottom part of the flesh looked ragged, like it was torn off the body.

"Ranger Washington later said, 'My heart was pounding in my chest so hard. I held my breath, stood perfectly still as the severed limb began to crawl into the woods but then stopped. The hand could feel the vibration of my heartbeats through the ground. It turned in my direction and crouched on the ground, like a lion. I slowly took a step backward. The hand pounced at me. Without thinking, I took my baton and hit the heavy hand into the fire ring. It grabbed the baton. I let the baton and the hand fall into the fire. I yelled "Help!" as I ran back to the car. I slid across the hood of the car, jumping into the open door.'

"The fire roared with the fresh body part.

"The fire softly hissed every time fresh blood landed on the embers, from the severed limb of the man faced down in front of the fire well. The seeping had slowed to a few drops sliding down the wall of the fire well.

"Ranger Washington heard sirens in the distance, and his nerves and confidence began to improve until he saw the hand crawl from the fire slowly, smoking, like it just left a warm sauna bath in winter. It walked on fingertips to the car, jumped onto his front passenger tire, and fell off. Then it jumped onto the front bumper, crawled onto the hood. At this point, Ranger Washington said he could hear the sirens at the entrance of the primitive campsite. Flashlights were coming through the woods from other campers. The hand tore off his wipers, scratched at the windshield on the passenger side, but it refused to attack the windshield by the Bible. Ranger Washington said that he moved the Bible around to keep the hand away until the police arrived. Ranger Washington lowered the driver-side window a little to tell the campers to leave, go back, and run. In one fluid movement, before he could yell 'Run!' the hand had leaped onto the roof of the car and reached a finger into the window. With its fingernail, it tore out a piece of flesh from the right top corner of Ranger Washington's mouth. Ranger Washington raised the window to trap the hand. Ranger Washington remembered feeling empowered. 'Yes, I got you, sucker!' he said.

"I arrived to find a horrified Ranger Washington trapped in his car. To the left in the car lights, I could see a roaring fire and something on the ground that looked like people. However, they did not hold my attention. Instead I stopped, and it felt like I had swallowed my heart. Literally it felt and tasted like I swallowed my heart. I could see Ranger Washington in the car, sliding from passenger side to driver side of the front seat. He was yelling for help. Before I could say anything, something that looked like a big, fat spider, something that resembled a tarantula jumped onto the car and moved with Ranger Washington from side to side. He tried to roll down the driver-side window a little and yell 'Go go go!' Other campers were coming through the woods. Ranger Washington looked behind his car and saw me on the bike. At this time, the spiderlike thing reached into the slightly open window and gouged out a piece of his jaw flesh. Ranger Washington rolled the window up and trapped the hand briefly.

"The rangers arrived moments before the ambulance, then others arrived—fire trucks and more rangers. I was frozen, paralyzed with fright. I did not know how to help—I just yelled for the other campers to run, stay back.

“Campers were standing with flashlights, paralyzed. No one knew what to do. The hand was trying to get free. The police and ambulance pulled up behind Ranger Washington’s car. Ranger Washington grabbed the Bible to touch the hand, but it was too strong. It broke the window, landed on the ground, crawled under the car. Ranger Washington said that he lost sight of the hand. After a bunch of screams and the arrival of the ambulance, it darted from under the car, across the head of the man faced down, across the middle of the fire, across the chest of the body behind the fire, and then off into the woods.

“The spiderlike thing waited under the car for a moment, waiting for Ranger Washington to get out. I yelled to Ranger Washington, ‘It’s under the car! Don’t get out!’ Only after feeling the multiple steps of the rangers and paramedics did the hand scurry away. The other campers yelled the location of the hand. The rangers and ambulance folk waited until they saw it crawl away across the bodies and fire.

“Ranger Washington said that he was not going to mention the nosebleed he got, nor the blood from the corners of his eyes as he wept blood. He must have been really spooked, the stress of that evening caused his blood pressure to rise quickly and remain elevated. His doctor said since that had never happened before or after this one occurrence, there was not much to worry about. However, as for the wound around the mouth, the doctor said it was a wound like the hospital had never seen and that it would not heal without surgery. To close the wound, the doctor had to cut off the seared surrounding flesh and stitched the wound close.

“Not wanting to sound stupid to state officials and the FBI and the local police, the next evening Ranger Washington took detailed pictures and made ceramic molds of the area to explain with proof that as the two men fought, their blood mixed and mingled with every glancing blow of the knife and the hatchet.

“Other campers in the closest campsite recalled hearing the friends laugh about their blood making the fire sizzle! Ranger Washington said that he was not sure if they were being truthful or just wanted to be in the nightly news. But he did know that the warm blood from the severed arm fed the fire! The burning flesh reignited the flames.

“I believe that because I saw it with my own eyes.

“According to the official police report, ‘Two male bodies were found in the primitive campsite area of Houston Woods. However, one of the victims’ hand was missing. It is believed a raccoon or some other animal dragged off the hand. The next morning, teams of people searched the campsite, woods, creek, and trees. The hand was never found.’

“After this incident, Ranger Washington stayed on at the campsite another two years. During that time, he realized the hand never left the campground. Because occasionally, he saw animals lying on the grounds with broken necks and crushed bodies. There were usually marks on the ground, indicating something being dragged.

“Ranger Washington said, ‘I noticed that most occurrences happen between 12:00 a.m. and

5:30 a.m. Most times, the tracks can be followed back to hollowed-out tree trunks. I have seen the hand only once since that unholy night. It was around 5:20 a.m."

"Ranger Washington said that he followed the hand back by the Indian mound area. There was a tall tree with an A-shaped opening in its base. The hand went into the opening. After sunrise, he returned to the tree and could see that soft root material had been thrown out and that the hand had bored into the ground under the tree. Ranger Washington said that he had never seen the hand during the day and guessed—more like hoped—that the sunlight would destroy it.

"Ranger Washington had hoped to never encounter or think about the hand again. Unfortunately, a few months before he quit working for the park, a child snuck out of his tent for a quick night bike ride, Row D of the non-primitive campsite area. The hand jumped into the spoke of the front wheel. Immediately the bike came to a halt, and the boy was thrown from the bike over the handlebars. He landed on the asphalt hard and fractured his collarbone. The hand, in one pounce, gained a firm grip across the boy's face, covering his nose and mouth. Unable to breathe in or exhale, the boy could feel his life silently slip away. If it was not for the commotion of the crashing bike and brief yelp as the boy fell from the bike, no one would have come to his rescue. Once the hand was surrounded, and folk throwing wood and chairs at it, the hand darted off across campsites, across the next row, and across the final set of campsites before entering the woods. There were women's screams and men's yells to 'Get it!' and 'Kill it!' The hand hurriedly scampered away deeper into the woods.

"Even now, the hand can be heard in the still of the night as it roams the grounds, looking for its long-removed body.

"The local police, state police, FBI, ministers, funeral directors, and others have met to discuss what to do about the hand. The conclusion was to offer precautions for all campers until a more permanent solution could be put into place:

- Watch out when going to the shower house at night. Go in pairs. The hand is extremely strong. It attacks by squeezing the neck, cutting off blood supply to the head, and you need more than one to help fight off and to yell for help. Little children especially need to travel in groups. The hand can cut off their ability to call for help by pinching their nose and covering their mouth at the same time.
- Zip tents from bottom to top at all times. A few months back, an unzipped tent led to a newborn being pulled from its tent by the ankle. Parents saved the crying child as it was being pulled from the tent. Even three months after that unholy night, the hand snuck into an unzipped tent shortly after sunset, around 9:00 p.m., and waited for occupants to return. After everyone started to quiet down and fall asleep, it tried to choke a teenager to death. Luckily, others woke up to help fight off the hand.

"Whenever the above rules are followed, there has never been an incident. Local officials used to give out brochures at the camp store with these precautions. The title used to include the catch phrase, 'Do not become a statistic while trying to be a hero.' Use the restroom before getting into the tent for the evening, walk in pairs, keep your tent zipped from bottom to top at *all* times.

"Ranger Washington said, before he quit working for the camp, he helped uproot many trees, helped to cut down and drag out trees in search of the hand. All efforts were unsuccessful. Eventually, Ranger Washington became confident that the hand would never be found and asked, 'If the hand is found, what can be done with it?' What could be done if the hand came after him while working alone? How do you kill something that is already dead? These questions are what led to his decision to stop working for the camp.

"When Mrs. Simpson, Ty, Tee, and I went by to see the site the next day, the police had it taped off with an armed guard protecting the campsite. There were so many specialists studying the site for evidence, possible causes, and for the missing hand. All campers were interviewed multiple times. Even when we returned home, we continued to get calls with questions from reporters and law officials."

Everyone around the campfire was quiet, mesmerized with eyes wide open, and hanging on to every word because at this very campground, someone was killed; not just one, but multiple killings in one night. They wondered what other secrets the campground held. Reading their eyes by a dying fire, I could make out the scared, the intrigued, and the curious thrill seekers. One of the teenagers put a log of pinewood into the fire.

"Everyone, look at the time." I reminded them to get ready to go to sleep. "It is getting late—it is already after midnight. Go to bed!"

The ones that were most exhausted entered the tents first; the ones with more energy inspected their tents, looking under air mattresses, sleeping bags, and clothes on the tent's floor before zipping up their tents.

The last girl, just before entering her tent, asked, "Mr. Simpson, can we go and see where it happened tomorrow?" I asked, "Do you mean later today?" Then I said, "Let us talk about it in the morning. The last time I visited the campsite in the primitive area H, it was not marked off as being a campsite anymore. I can show you the area where the site used to be. If you are interested, we can ride bikes over there—I remember exactly how to get to it."

Then other voices came through the tent walls. "I want to go also." "Me too." "I'm going."

After a few more minutes, the remaining campers retired to their tents while I remained by the fire to make sure it was put out properly.

The rustling and mumbling from each tent subsided quickly as each person dozed off. The boys tried to be tough and act like they were not afraid. However, I noticed they were the most secured and had zipped the tent door from the floor all the way to the roof. I had to stop them from using a shoestring to tie the zipper shut for safety reasons and I would not be able to get into the tent.

The intrigued and the curious thrill seekers among us looked forward to visiting the campsite area H.

I was alone with my thoughts, as the sounds of sleeping bags' zippers and tents' zippers closed up their occupants for the night and as the sounds of popping embers sharpened my memories of that horrible weekend so many years ago. I realize there are so many questions that have gone unanswered for years; even today, there are questions that were never asked that I would like to know the answers to and hope that Keef can fill in the gaps.

Forty-five minutes later, I turned in for the night.

Seemingly 7:15 a.m. came early; after waking late, the sun was already peeking through the trees. Other campers were out walking their dogs. Others were piling dry kindling into small tepee piles inside their fire well; others were twisting old newspapers into knots and soaking them with lighter fluid before piling on the kindling and small pieces of wood to start their morning fires.

I forgot to put the food away last night; raccoons had pizza boxes pulled onto the ground inside the food tent, and pizza crust spread all over our campsite. A loaf of bread had been torn open and partially eaten; some slices of bread were found between the girls' tent and the campsite behind us.

Around 8:35 a.m., a parent dropped off a girl who could not spend a night due to her faith. The other girls had expected her and left a vacant sleeping bag for her by the entrance of the tent. Mia barely said "Good morning" as she made her way to the girls' tent. I spent a few minutes talking with her mother and invited her to some coffee or breakfast. She accepted, parked the car, and took a seat at the campfire. Ms. Medina stoked the fire for me while I fixed the coffee. We laughed as I pointed to the mess the raccoons made. She helped walk around and pick up food. After getting toast and coffee, Ms. Medina had to leave around 9:20.

A few minutes later, another parent dropped off a boy who could not travel with us yesterday. "Good morning, Mr. Farnham, would you like something to eat or coffee?" I asked.

Mr. Farnham replied, "No, I need to go and get my grandchildren for the weekend," then he was on his way. He stopped and backed his truck up and then asked, "What time do I need to pick him up tomorrow?" I replied, "Around two o'clock." "Thanks." Again, he was on his way.

"Well, young man, are you hungry?" I asked. He said, "No, thank you."

"If you are thirsty or hungry, there is food in the blue tent." Jesse got an apple and sat around the fire.

After getting the morning fire going and cleaning up the area, I set out the milk, juice, fruit, and cereal. Then boiled water for hot chocolate and, in another pot, boiled a baker's dozen of eggs. Lastly, I cooked some sausage patties. Once the smell of the sausage started to permeate the tents' walls, the campers started mumbling and moving in the tents; a few minutes later, there were a few draggy words—*morning, good morning*—as the children started to exit the tents. By 10:30 most had washed up and eaten breakfast.

Some boys were throwing the football and meeting other kids. Some girls were riding bikes while others were still in the shower house. Everyone else was sitting around the campfire, trying to wake up.

I asked, "Who is going to help me clean up?" Silence! Surprisingly, no one answered. I assumed they were too full from breakfast. I volunteered everyone under the sound of my voice with tasks, to help expedite the cleanup of our campsite.

While I finished cleaning up the food tent after breakfast, I yelled to the campers "Go and straighten up your tents" and reminded them to spread the word, "All of us are expected to meet around the campfire in thirty minutes—at 11:05. Now go and finish getting ready for the day!"

I reminded the campers once more "to return by 11:05 a.m. for a meeting, and when you return, know the following: what events you are doing today, how you will get to and from the events, and how long you will be at the event. Now go!"

They regrouped mostly on time. "All gather around! Is everyone here?" I reminded everyone to welcome Mia and Jesse.

While everyone was around the campfire, I prayed for everyone's safety and for all of us to have fun. We all said "Amen!"

"Now, let me set the ground rules. No one is to be alone, go with someone else from our group at all times no matter your age, be respectful of other campers and yourself, and lastly, if you visit the camp store, only three maximum of our group is to be in the store at the same time.

"In the next twenty minutes, before you go to any event, I need each of you to tell me (1) what events you are planning to do today, (2) how you plan on getting to and from the events, and (3) how long you will be at the event. In the food tent, I will update the whiteboard with your name, place, and return times. Let me remind you, we are here to have fun, so represent your families well, and you better not make me come looking for you! If the whiteboard says you are to return by 1:30, I suggest you be early and arrive at 1:25, not at 1:35. The first time you are late, I will plan the rest of your activities this weekend. No excuses will be accepted!"

While I had everyone's attention, I asked, "Are there any questions?" One child said yes. "What if we go to the next event late, will we get into trouble?"

"Good question, let me clarify. After each event, you must return to the campsite before going to the next event. I need to know that you are okay—so plan your time accordingly. Additionally, I will have lunch ready at 1:00 p.m., dinner ready or in progress by 6:00 p.m. Everyone has to be back at the campsite before 6:05 p.m. If you want to go someplace after that, we will go together as a group."

I asked again, "Are there any questions?" There were no additional questions. My last comments were "Remember you are a child of God, so act like it" and "Have fun."

Little groups started to form immediately; a few minutes later, the whiteboard had the first scheduled events for the day. Before long, the whiteboard had basketball, the beach, bike rental, Putt-Putting, and tour of the Indian mound scheduled.

A question was asked, “Mr. Simpson, are we still going to the campsite for the hand?” I said, “Yes, if you still want to.”

“Can we go after dinner, just before nightfall?” I got a quick push back.

“No no no, not at night.”

“Can we go around 3:00 p.m.?”

I agreed, “Okay, let’s add it as an event.”

Mia asked the question, “What is the hand?”

I asked, “Can one of you tell Mia and Jesse about the hand?” My hour-long story from the previous night was reduced to a fifteen-minute answer and three different versions. But they got the gist of the story.

I reminded everyone, “Before leaving, please air out your tents, just open your windows and allow a breeze to pass through, and zip your tent doors close completely from the floor to the roof.”

Shortly after the prayer and our meeting, the campsite was empty with the children going to their scheduled events. I started preparing the food tent for lunch and finished picking up around the campsite before returning to the dying fire.

Finally, I have time to think.

I do not think I ever sent a sympathy or a get-well card to Mr. Keef; wish that I had. I wonder if Keef ever found out who the men were. Why did one of the slain men have frogs in his pocket? How did the men arrive at the campsite? I noticed there was not a vehicle at their campsite. Why had someone dug multiple holes around the base of the Indian mound that night?

I drove around Houston Woods in a deliberate path to see if my campers had arrived at their events safely and to drop off bottles of water and fruit.

Some of the boys were playing basketball with other campers (I offered the other ball players bottles of water); some girls were playing volleyball with other campers (I offered the other players bottles of water). Some of the younger teenage campers were playing in the sand and splashing beach water. I left hand sanitizers and bottles of water for them. I did not see some of the older campers in the tree shade by the sailboats until I caught a glimpse of them in my rearview mirror as I pulled away. I was out of water anyway and would give them water when I return.

After giving out my last bottle of water, I left the campgrounds. I was on my way to the store to purchase cases of water and other needed supplies. I passed Mr. Keef’s house. I looked to see if he was out. “I doubt it since it is in the middle of the day.” The wood pile’s levels had been restored from the previous day, but Keef was not sitting out in the heat. I would return for wood around 5:00 p.m. I kept driving to the nearest superstore with a market, which was not very far away (at the beginning of Todd Road).

The first item I grabbed was water, three cases of twenty-ounce bottles of water, then a rope for a hike, extra toothbrushes, and extra bars of soap, snacks, graham crackers, large marshmallows, box of chocolate, skewers, and the last things I grabbed are large bags of ice.

While pushing my cart in search of a short line at the cash register, I noticed a familiar face restocking shelves in the cosmetics row. I pushed my heavy cart to the side briefly and walked over and said hello.

Mr. Keef paused briefly and said hello. I said, “I don’t want to keep you from work, just wanted to stop by and say hello.” He said, “Thanks, how is the camping trip going?”

“It is going well, we have burned up almost all our wood.” I smiled.

Smiling, he said, “Run up and stop by the house, the missus is there.”

I said, “I will later, now I need to get back to the campsite. What time do you get off work today?”

“They have me working part-time as needed, today I am scheduled to get off around 4:00 p.m.,” replied Keef.

I decided to invite Keef to dinner. “You and your wife are welcomed to the campsite tonight, and we’re planning to have dinner at 6:00 p.m. We should be back before then. We won’t be hard to find, we are a few campsites down from the shower house in Row D with three large tents, and the big, blue food tent is in the middle.”

Mr. Keef asked, “You will be returning from where?”

Curiously, I asked, “What do you mean?”

Keef replied, “You mentioned that you would be back before dinner.”

I said, “Oh, yeah. A few of the campers want to visit the old campsite where the hand incident happened. We planned to walk over to the primitive area around 3:00 p.m. and should be back by 5:00 p.m.”

Keef mentioned that his wife was not likely to join him, but he would come by for a visit and also would bring a few pieces of wood, then he said, “Hard—and softwood,” winked and smiled at me, as if to say “I know how you like your campfire wood.”

I replied, “Great and thanks. I look forward to seeing you tonight around 6:00 p.m.” I grabbed my shopping cart and checked out at the nearest counter.

I drove around Houston Woods in reversed order, dropping off more water and seeing if my campers were okay or needed anything.

The older teenagers were walking along the beach; bottles of water were left for them. The younger teenagers and one of the volleyball girls were ready to return to the campsite and prepare for their next event. The boys were finished playing basketball. I was about to pass them at the camp store when I saw two of the boys waiting for their turn to go inside. One boy had almost finished a red Popsicle. They waved me down. I stopped and said, “Hello, are you okay?” The boy with red lips and tongue said that he was glad to see me and jumped into the van. I thought the other boys were okay and going to walk back to the campsite to relax for a few minutes before going to their next event. I could barely hear them over the chatty teenagers in the van who were also talking to them out the back windows.

Well at least, I had plenty of help to get the food out of the van and to help put the drinks on ice. We turned left to drive up the hill, then around the circle down to our campsite.

Some teenagers had already fixed themselves some lunch. I could tell by the food tent being unzipped, bags of chips being open on the table, the cooler lids not being completely closed, and an open can of juice on the ground beside a chair around the campfire well. My teenage campers in the van helped to get the food into the tent and coolers, washed their hands, and then fixed themselves some lunch. The others arrived back and lunch continued.

As expected, the fruits and vegetables were lasting longer than the sweet cakes and chips.

I updated the whiteboard in the tent for the afternoon activities. Everyone seemed to be on schedule. The campsite was empty; this time most of my campers were out doing things close to the campsite. A couple of them went to play Putt-Putt, some were riding bikes, and some were just walking around the campground. Someone was in their tent napping, and a couple of the campers were up by the shower house.

The soft warm breeze felt so nice. On the bench of the camp table, inside of the food tent, I lay down to read a few pages of a book and dozed off for a while. I awoke around 2:50 when my older campers arrived at the food tent for drinks, snacks, food, and fruit. Voices asked, "Are you ready, Mr. Simpson?"

Wow, I must have dozed off. I picked my book up off the ground and said, "I really needed that nap."

The question was repeated, "Are we still going to the campsite for the hand?"

Before answering, I put some water on my hand from my water bottle and splashed it onto my face. A little more coherent now, I replied, "How many people are going?" I asked another question, "Is everyone here? Let me get organized. Let me update the whiteboard."

I called out names and got replies, here, here, here. Then I looked at the next planned event; almost everyone wanted to go to the campsite where the hand incident took place. "Get the other campers to find out what they are planning to do so I can update the whiteboard. We do not have enough bikes for everyone. It is a good walking distance from here, so everyone will need to put on some comfortable walking shoes."

The older campers spoke up quickly and said, "Mr. Simpson, can we all just jump into the van because we just walked all the way back from the beach, past the camp store, up the hill, down, down our row to get to the campsite. We are too tired!"

"I don't think we can get everyone into the van."

The boys quickly said, "We can fold the seats into the floor of the van, and everyone can stand up in the back of the van."

I said, "If you can show me this can be done safely, we can try it. In the meantime, what are you other campers going to do while we're at the campsite where the hand incident took place?"

They replied, "I want to go too. I want to go."

"Then perfect, we are all going!"

The teenagers opened all the side doors and the hatchback, removed all items from the van seats, folded the chairs down into the floor, and said, "There is plenty of room in the van. We could probably squeeze an extra five people into the van." We all laughed.

At 3:05 we started the van-packing experiment. I turned on the air conditioning and used the buttons to close the passenger-side door. There was not a problem; everyone was almost in the van. I used the next button to close the driver-side door; there was not a problem. I asked, "Is everyone in?" They said yes. I pressed the last button to close the hatchback. The van was loaded. Everyone was elated that their plan and teamwork proved to be successful without any modifications.

I started to roll away from our campsite very slowly. Someone in the back started to softly chant "slow rollin'," heads bobbing "slow rollin'." Everyone started singing along in excitement. "Slow rollin'." I laughed and embarrassingly said, "You all are crazy." Other campers looked on as our low-riding van rolled by with teenagers chanting "Slow rollin'."

I turned right at the circle and let the van roll down the hill and around the curve. At the bottom of the hill behind the camp store, I signaled to turn left. Everyone looked out of the left-side windows and saw the sign for primitive camping. I slowly turned left; soon there was nothing on either side of the street but trees. The only connection to the non-primitive area is the camp store out the hatchback window, even that was leaving our view quickly.

A question from the back, "Mr. Simpson, is this the way you rode your bike?"

"Yes, there was some moonlight that night. Truthfully, I did not realize how far away the primitive camp was because it was my first time ever coming to this section. All I knew is that someone needed help and that I could not turn back." It was really dark, the darkness itself felt thick and cool.

Turn after turn, the drive became creepier. The next question from the back, "Why would anyone want to camp in this area?" My reply was, "Some people enjoy this type of camping."

We arrived at an empty opening of depressed-looking campsites and turned left toward the H section. After passing a portable toilet on my left, a little ways down, I pulled up to where the campsite used to be and stopped the van in almost the same spot that Mr. Keef had parked his car.

"We are here," I said and then used the buttons to open the side doors and the hatchback.

Immediately, I noticed the empty vastness of the primitive camping area. There is not a single camper here today. Even with the sun high in the sky, the campsite seemed desolate and felt sad. The campsite was overgrown and seemed to have been neglected. I was sure it was by design; the state park organization probably wanted this site to be erased from the park's memory. Despite the neglect, nothing seemed to want to grow there. I could still make out the layout of the campground. To the right, there was a winding stream; ahead and to the left was the large hill that comes down from behind the Indian mound. It was the same hill that other campers came down from that night with flashlights. The fire well was missing, but overall the campsite area was as I remembered; however, it seemed to be a lot smaller than I remember.

Jesse asked, "Mr. Simpson, where was the hand?"

"It was everywhere," I replied. Pointing in front of us and slightly to the left, "That is the hill where five to seven campers with flashlights were navigating."

I turned back behind us and pointed to the right and said, "I was on my bike over there, with my heart beating hard in my chest. I arrived a few minutes before the ranger."

I turned more to the left and pointed a little ways behind the van and commented, "There is where the first ranger car slid to a stop, and immediately behind it was the first ambulance."

A few more inches to the left, I pointed to our van. "That is where Mr. Keef's car was parked." With another turn to the left, we completed surveying the campsite that night. I walked forward and pointed to the area where the fire well was. I pointed out, "There is where the first body was faced down, and the right arm was missing a hand. The place where the hand belonged was squirting blood into the fire. With every drop of blood, I recognized a familiar sound, the same sound you hear after pouring water to extinguish a fire." The campers were taken aback with the details. I could hear "Aww," "Eww," "Yuk," "That is nasty," and "Cool." I apologized, "I am sorry, I got caught up in the details."

The older teens said, "No, go ahead, Mr. Simpson. We're okay."

I asked, "Are y'all sure? If some of you do not want to hear any more details, you can go sit in the van. I left the air condition on." No one left; however, they are huddled together noticeably closer.

I made big sideways steps to the left, as though I was walking around and behind an imaginary fire well (the campers moved with me); then I pointed, "There is where the body was lying face up with the left hand cooking over the fire. I could smell the burning flesh before arriving."

A question came, "What did it smell like?"

I said, "Actually, it smelled like bacon." The campers had mixed reactions and emotions, some laughed while others were grossed out.

We stopped, now facing the van. I pointed to the van and said, "Ranger Washington's car was there, and he had his headlights shining onto this area." I turned to the point behind us and said, "Campers were using flashlights and lanterns, trying to get down the hill to this campsite."

I turned back to face the van and continued to say, "The campers saw the hand crawl over to Ranger Washington's car. They saw the hand follow Ranger Washington to the passenger side and try to climb onto the hood of the car by jumping onto the front passenger wheel. After a few unsuccessful attempts to get onto the hood, the hand returned to the front of the car, then climbed onto the chrome bumper, up the grill, and onto the hood of the car. That is when I saw the hand."

While still facing the van, I moved to the right, behind some of the kids, to walk over to the spot where I was standing with my bike that night. My campers followed me closely. A few minutes later, we had arrived to the exact spot. I turned back to regain the same vantage point that I had the night of the hand incident. I pointed to the van and said, "I saw the hand jump on the hood of Ranger Washington's car, and he was inside the car, yelling. He was on the front seat, sliding from side to side. To me he should be recognized as being a hero because other campers may have been hurt if he hadn't tried to warn us to turn back and run. In the moment, Ranger Washington rolled down his car window and yelled "Go go" to the campers who were more than halfway down the hill and to me, the hand had ripped a chunk of flesh off his face, leaving a cauterized hole at that spot."

A question came, "Are you talking about the man who sold us wood yesterday?"

"Yes," I replied.

Another question came, "Is that why he had the scar on his face?"

"Yes, the hand is what scarred his face."

Another question came from the newcomer Jesse, "What happened to the hand?" Mia followed up another question immediately, "Where is the hand?"

I replied, "For both questions, the answer is the same—I don't know. The last time I had seen the hand, it had broken Ranger Washington's driver-side window and crawled up under his car. Then it crossed the body that was faced down. It crawled across the middle of the hot fire, then crawled across the chest of the body that was faced up behind the fire well, and then darted off into the woods over there." I pointed to a swath of woods alongside the creek.

I reminded everyone that time is passing. "This is where the hand incident took place. Now, we need to be getting back—some of you have events scheduled for 4:30."

Without delay, we repacked the van and rolled away. Before exiting the primitive camping area, the youngest campers said, "I did not like that campsite." There were no other comments as we returned to the street behind the camp store and turned right to go up the hill to our camping area.

Once we reached the top of the hill, some of the campers wanted to get out of the van to find out the time and name of the free movie to be shown this evening. I stopped; half of the campers got out of the van. The remaining campers and I returned to the campsite.

When the van doors were opened, the campers went off in many different directions. A couple of the campers went to the shower house to use the restroom, a girl disappeared into her tent, and a couple of boys jumped onto bikes and raced off into the direction of the other teenagers at the movie site.

Fifteen minutes later, more campers returned to the campsite, then went to their next event after reviewing and updating the whiteboard. Occasionally, I got the hurried question "What is for dinner?" My quick reply was "You will see at 6:00 p.m."

Dinner should go quickly; all I needed to do was set out the empanacha packets that we made on Thursday (two days ago). We made up the word *empanacha* to mean to wrap for cooking. The concept is borrowed from empanadas; the only difference was that we were wrapping food in aluminum foil instead of bread.

Thursday night, some of the campers helped to make a variety of empanachas. We had a good time! We put on a comedy movie to watch while mixing up fourteen pounds of hamburger with different combinations of ingredients, pulling off corn husks and removing little strings between the rows of corn, cutting slices of cheese into half-inch strips.

LJ and Mia mixed half of the hamburger with diced onions, celery, carrots, salt-and-pepper, and ketchup.

Naya slowed the progress when she decided to bake cookies; we needed the roller. All was forgiven with each bite of the cookies. The kitchen smelled good.

Reena and Jesse mixed the other half of the hamburger with cream of mushroom, mixed vegetables, and random mild seasonings.

Naya and her mother rolled four ears of corn into warm melted butter until they were fully coated with butter. Then placed four ears beside each other on aluminum foil, and an ice cube for each ear of corn was added. Then all sides of the empanacha packet were sealed so that moisture could not get into or out of the packet. Immediately the corn empanacha was placed into the deep freezer. This was repeated to create five packets with four ears of corn.

Another teenager and I measured out a little more than a half-pound of hamburger mixture with ketchup and placed it on the center of a chopping board, then used the roller to flatten the mixture. Next we took the mixture and placed it into their hands and formed it into a rectangle shape and then placed it onto a sheet of aluminum foil. Then we pressed three strips of cheese softly into the hamburger, then we folded the aluminum foil and sealed the edges to seal in the moisture. Finally, Reena and Mia put the empanacha into the deep freezer once they finished creating an airtight seal. This process was repeated to create twelve packets.

LJ and Jesse measured out a little more than a half-pound of hamburger mixture with cream of mushroom and placed it directly onto the aluminum foil. Next they used their hands and formed the mixture into a rectangle shape. Then they folded the aluminum foil and sealed the edges to seal in the moisture. Finally, Reena and Mia put their empanachas into the deep freezer as they were completed. This process was repeated to create twelve packets.

Mrs. Simpson washed and wrapped a couple of white and sweet potatoes in aluminum foil and put them into the refrigerator, just in case someone would want one.

I used my last few pieces of kindling and logs of wood to start the fire. Reena and her sister drove down to the camp store to get a bundle of wood. When they returned, I put half of the bundle into the fire well.

It was 6:00 p.m. I was very pleased with myself. I had a roaring fire with good embers; all the empanachas were on the table along with sliced and diced lettuce, tomatoes, shredded cheese, sour cream, butter spread, and a lemon cake that was purchased from the local superstore. The marshmallows and graham crackers were visible in the back of the tent but not accessible.

While waiting in the food tent for the campers to arrive, I saw them approaching and reminded them to wash their nasty hands. I went ahead and placed the corn empanachas into the fire so that they would be ready when the individual empanachas were done or for campers to have as an appetizer.

Around 6:30 some of my campers were starting to come out of the shower house and were walking back to the campsite. A couple of campers were already sitting around the campfire, watching their empanachas.

Off in the distance, I could see a small truck rolling down our row, pausing for little children to move out of the way before rolling over their chalk drawings; immediately after the truck passed, the children resumed drawing. The truck kept approaching; some other children paused throwing the football and waited for the truck to pass before resuming throwing. As the truck passed the shower house, I heard the chirping sound of the driver putting a foot on the brakes. Then I heard Naya say, "Hello, Mr. Washington."

"Good evening," he replied. I continued to look on; it was Keef. I forgot that he was going to join us tonight for dinner. I waved him down as he turned into the parking spot next to the van. There's a lot of laughter and activity in the campground. There were many campers, many children, and many activities going on in the park. The campground was lively.

I walked over and greeted Keef as he was getting out of the truck. While exchanging pleasantries, he reached onto the back of his truck and handed me a few logs of oak wood, and then he grabbed a few more logs and walked over to the campfire. I said, "Thanks for the wood." He replied, "There is more where that came from," and then pointed to the back of his truck, which was full of wood.

I said, "Grab a seat," then asked, "What are you drinking: warm water, chilled water, water on the rocks, or a fruit juice pouch?"

He wittily replied, "With so many choices, I am going with chilled water," and laughed.

I returned to the food tent. Repeatedly, I heard "Hi, Mr. Washington" as campers returned to the campsite again. "Hi, Mr. Washington." I had one of the campers take Keef a cold bottle of water while I grabbed a mitten, tongs, and pan to remove the corn empanachas from the fire and to make room for new empanachas. I then placed four baked potatoes into the embers.

I returned to the fire. The only seat available was at an angle to Keef. Some of the campers were leaning over the fire to watch their empanachas. I asked, "Why don't you guys sit down?"

They replied, "There's no place to sit, all the chairs are taken."

Keef said, "I have some chairs in the front seat of the truck. Can you boys open the passenger door and get the three chairs out? Perfect, everyone at the campfire, have a seat."

"Thanks, Mr. Washington."

I explained to Mr. Washington, "You have a variety of options for dinner tonight: salad with blue cheese, ranch, or Italian dressing; a cheese burger empanacha; cream of mushroom empanacha; baked potato, white or sweet; and a full complement of water, chips, fruit, or lemon cake. Also, there is another fifteen minutes or so, on your empanachas." *I am letting him have the empanachas I put into the fire for myself. I will start a couple of new empanachas. Hopefully it will seem like I remembered that he was coming to dinner!*

Mr. Keef asked, "What is an empanacha?" I explained to him how we created our own word to mean food that is combined and wrapped inside of aluminum foil and cooked in an open fire. He replied, "That is very similar to what I used to do in the Boy Scouts."

I asked, "How long were you in the Boy Scouts?"

Keef replied, "All the way through the twelfth grade, but I never achieved Eagle Scout."

I confessed, "Me too, I was in the Scouts from the sixth grade to the tenth grade. Likewise, I never completed the requirements for Eagle Scout. I also helped out with the Webelos."

Keef said, "I remember them, isn't that what you became after being a Cub Scout?"

"Yes, the Webelos help the Cub Scouts become a Boy Scout," I commented.

Keef asked, "Did you get to wear the bands around your arm?"

I excitedly replied, "Yes, around the shoulder." It was great talking with someone else who understands the Scouts. Then, almost on cue, we both held up three fingers and started repeating the Boy Scouts Oath.

"On my honor I will do my best, to do my duty to God and my country and to obey the Scout Law; to help other people at all times; to keep myself physically strong, mentally awake, and morally straight."[1]

The embarrassed moans and groans were too much to hold in; we burst out laughing loudly. Halfway through the Boys Scouts Oath, we heard, "No way," "I can't believe it," "Unbelievable," "This is embarrassing!" "My god, how long is it?" "Embarrassing!" It was too funny, none of the teenagers wanted to be seen with us. Even my support group chimed in, "Dad, please don't ever do that again." Keef and I laughed and laughed so hard. Even the campers behind our campsite stood up and gave us the thumbs up and said, "Our son is in the Boy Scouts." Then my campers said in unison, "Oh no." Keef and I were laughing so hard, tears were running down our faces.

Some of my best camping memories started with the Scouts. It was really nice to have that in common.

I told Keef, "The idea for empanachas may have come from the Scouts. I do not remember what we called them when I was in the Boy Scouts."

Trying to stop laughing, Keef asked the campers, "Did you all have a good time today?"

Everyone excitedly said, "Yes, and we're going to see a movie tonight up in the circle."

Keef asked, “What movie are they showing tonight?”

No one knew; some of the campers said, “The sign in the circle did not give a movie name—just said a family Disney movie will be shown at 9:00 p.m. After sunset.”

Keef looked around and then commented, “This part of the park has not changed much through the years.”

I agreed, “It is still a great place to bring family and friends for a weekend camping trip.”

Keef said, “It looks like you have picked out the best campsite in this area. It is pretty flat and does not have any rolling hills, this is a good spot for a campsite.”

I thanked him and said, “I agree, the one across the road is pretty good.” Keef and some of the campers looked.

Keef said, “It is pretty good, yes, that’s not bad.”

Some of the younger campers went bike riding. A couple others threw a Frisbee with campers further down Row D.

The father and son from the campsite behind ours came over and introduced themselves. “Hello, we are the Thompsons. This is my son, Mark. He is the one I mentioned is a Boy Scout.” Embarrassed, Mark said hello. The chuckles and giggles started again.

I said, "I apologize, my campers are not laughing at you. They are laughing because they were embarrassed when two older guys were chanting the Boy Scout Oath. And we made it sound *good*!" Mark and his father then laughed. "Please have a seat, join us for a minute." Then I asked, "Do either of you want anything to drink or to snack on? We have lemon cake."

They both replied, "No, thank you. Our dinner will be ready shortly."

Some of the older teens were trying to decide if they wanted to walk down to the camp store and get some snacks to sneak into the movie. When Keef asked everyone "What did you all do today?" some said, "So much that we do not remember," "Spent time at the beach," "Played volleyball," "Mr. Simpson took us to the campsite where the hand incident happened," or "Rode bikes down to the fishing stream."

LJ asked, "Dad, do you have any matches?"

"Why?"

"The family across the street is having a problem starting their fire because their matches are wet."

"Are you going to help them to start the fire?"

LJ said, "Sure."

"Then come and get them." I gave him some newspaper, a cigarette lighter, matches, kindling, and lighter fluid.

Mark volunteered to go with him. Mark said, "I'm real good at starting a fire." Fifteen minutes later, we saw smoke, then a fire. The boys walked back over to our fire, giving each other a high five. Behind them was a voice, saying, "Thank you very much." The boys both looked back and said with proud smiles of accomplishment, "You are welcome, sir. No problem, anytime."

Back at our fire, LJ and Mark said, "Mr. Hampton was never going to get the fire going. He was trying to start the fire with large pieces of wood drenched with lighter fluid. It looks like he had fifty matches in the fire well."

Mr. Thompson, Keef, and I smiled and agreed that Mr. Hampton would still be trying to get their fire going if it were not for the boys.

I put another piece of hardwood onto the fire. Most of the teenagers have returned with new friends. Cold fruit drink pouches, a slice of cake, and couple of bottles of water were given away. While their new friends were waiting for refreshments, I said hello to the new faces; they said hello.

Mr. Keef asked, "Did you have fun today?" With sweaty faces, they said yes.

Mr. Thompson asked, "What is the most interesting thing you did today?"

One said, "I went on a hike and saw a baby black bear on the other side of the creek."

Keef said, "Yes, we have bears here. You need to be very careful of them. If you can see the babies, then the mother is very close by."

Another child said, "Dad and I rented a boat to go fishing, but we did not catch anything—all day."

Mia said, "I think the campsite where the hand incident happened was the most exciting."

Mr. Thompson laughed and said, "Are they still telling that old story?"

One of the new faces said, "My father told me about that story years ago. I think he said something about two guys fighting and one guy had a hand cut off and that a bear ate it."

Mr. Keef looked horrified and said, "That is not what happened, is it Mr. Simpson?"

A motherly voice from behind our tents said, "Frank, Mark, dinner is ready!"

Mr. Thompson said, "Just a minute, dear. Come over and say hello."

The reply was, "I will be there shortly."

I replied, "No, Keef, that is not what happened at all! Keef, I have some questions about that night that still trouble me. You may have the answers or know where I can get the answers. Do you mind if I ask you some questions about that night?"

He thought for a moment and said, "I am not sure if I will have any answers but will tell you what I know."

"I have always wondered how the men arrived to the primitive campsite. I do not recall there being a vehicle at their campsite."

Keef replied, "That is a good question, the ranger assumed the men hiked to Houston Woods—which is odd in itself. I have never heard of anyone hiking to the campground."

"Who were the men? Were they related?"

Keef said, "No, they were not related, but they were a very odd pair. One was a twenty-seven-year-old student of archeology from some college up north, he was in the doctorate program. Four months prior, he had returned from an excavation in South America. Apparently, he was touring state parks in America, because just ten days earlier, he was sighted in Texas alone in the Sabine National Forest. The other man was soft-spoken. He built wood furniture, had no children, lived alone, and was a very proud Shawnee native of the Chillicothe, Ohio, area. Police reports stated that both of his parents were Shawnee—the father was very spiritual, and the mother was a little peculiar and very quiet."

Mrs. Thompson had walked over to remind her family that their dinner is ready. I smiled and introduced myself.

Mr. Thompson asked, "Are you telling us the missing hand story is true?"

Keef replied, "It depends on which version of the story you heard."

I asked, "Is it true that one of the men had frogs in his pocket?"

A boy took a bite of cake and laughed and said, "Frogs?" Some faces had smiles while other faces were unresponsive.

Keef said, "Now that was crazy. I have not been able to make any sense of that. It was so bizarre because one pocket had dead dry frogs, another pocket had small frogs that were still alive and crawling around and when he fell and crushed a green frog with very big yellow eyes, which is not even a species that is found in this country."

A question was asked, "What did law enforcement say about the frogs?"

Keef responded, "The FBI report was inconclusive, they tried to link the multiple holes dug around the base of the Indian mound to the guys searching for frogs. I am not sure of whom or what dug the holes."

I asked, "Was there anything found on the men that could have come from the holes? Like bones, cloth, teeth, trinkets?"

Keef replied, "I am not sure, why do you ask?"

I replied, "I have a theory!"

Keef said, "There is one more thing, it was not found on the FBI report, it was on the ranger's report. The report mentioned that bones were found around the fire, they assumed the men had dropped the bones from dinner."

A camper said, "So when the man fell, he killed a frog?"

Keef said, “Yes, there was something else about the frogs. Some of the frogs had their mouths stitched closed, both dead frogs and living frogs. Those guys were crazy. The frogs were dissected, and inside of their mouths were found human remains, mostly fingernails, hair, eyelashes, saliva-soaked raisins.”

Some girls said, “Aww that is so sad.”

Some other campers said, “That is gross and that had to be painful for the frogs.”

I reminded everyone, “The movie is starting in ten minutes.” No one moved. Keef asked for more wood from the back of his truck. Two pieces of hardwood were added to the fire.

“Was there anything else odd about them?”

Keef thought for a minute and said, “Besides the fact that neither of them had on shoes, no. The odd thing about this is that their feet and pants were very muddy, and their shoes were neatly paired and found by the street. The ambulance driver recalls driving over the shoes when they arrived to the site.” Then Keef commented, “Mr. Simpson, you passed them that night when you turned off the street.”

I said, “Yes, I saw three pairs of footwear: sneakers, boots, and moccasins. I quickly forgot about them when I arrived and saw you in the car calling, yelling for help.”

There is silence around the campfire; some neighboring campers that were en route to the movie had stopped to listen to the details for the night of the hand incident.

“Two more questions, Keef. Did anyone find odd things in the tree branches, like worms or morsels of food near the edge of the woods? Did you find morsels of food that had been placed on something, not directly on the ground, or food in a mousetrap or any other bizarre ways of keeping food off the ground?”

With cutting eyes, Keef looked at me hard and long, then said, “No one knew that. How did you know someone was feeding the animals that night? Why do you ask the question?”

All eyes shifted to me with skepticism, awaiting my reply. I gathered my composure from the implicating question and measuredly said, “I did not know, you just confirmed a theory of mine that can make sense of the events that took place that night.”

Keef said with a crack in his voice, “I would love to hear what you have come up with because for many years now, I cannot close this chapter in my life because nothing seems to make sense.”

I commented, “Keef, the next question is very important, please think back to all the police reports and to your experiences that night. Are you 100 percent sure there were only two men at that campsite that night? Your answer will determine if my theory holds water or not.”

All eyes shifted back to Keef as he paused between each answer. “I do not think so. I did not see anyone. It has been a long time, I do not remember. I would need to reread some of the early reports. I am not 100 percent sure.”

I commented, “It would be nice to know if anyone investigated the other side of the creek and what they found if anything.” I said, “Keef, to answer your question, about the morsels of food—I only asked a question that a very insightful woman asked me and I did not have the answer.”

For years, the hand incident has tormented me; I have retold the story of that night many times across the years. About ten years ago, in the woods of Verona, North Carolina, along the shores of Stones Bay, I repeated the story to a gathering crowd, a night before a big family reunion. There was an older woman who was blind. The young folk had such great love for her; they helped her to a bench along the edge of the shore with tree branches shielding her from the rays of the setting sun. After the story, the crowd went different ways. I asked if could help her back to the house. She said, “I am not ready to go in just yet.” I commented on how comfortable it felt along the shore and sat on the sand beside her bench. We could hear children behind us jumping out from behind things and growling, “The hand is going to get you,” then immediately the scream of a scared child and laughter. I asked, “What did you think of the story?”

She said, “Protect your soul because multiple souls had to be lost in your story!” She asked, “You are a God-fearing man, aren’t you?”

“Yes, Mama,” I replied.

She said, “I can feel the goodness in you.”

Not wanting to be pushy, I put a smile on my face that she could not see and asked, “What do you mean multiple souls had to be lost in my story?”

She paused to spit out some snuff into a can and then continued to so say, “The story you told is one of consequences, when you do not protect your soul. The men in the story should not have played around with something they could not control—at minimum, there needed to be three men, four would have been better.”

“What do you mean?”

She said, “As sure as I know there is a fly on your shoulder, those men were playing with darkness without fully understanding the consequences of their movements, words, and thoughts.”

“How do you know this from the story?” I asked. “How do you know I did not make the entire story up for your enjoyment?”

The woman turned her face into my direction and proceeded to tell me a story about her life. “As a child, I remember sitting in the kitchen and listening to my grandmother tell my mother different incantations. She always started off with teaching the counter-curse. Once that was mastered, she taught the power of the curse, then she taught the proper time to use the curse. My mother had to master this before Grandma would teach her how to execute the curse. Grandma would never allow my mother or me to write down the incantations because they were too dangerous and others could use them on us. It now seems like a very wise practice, now that I have lost my eyesight.

“My grandmother learned the art from my great-grandmother as my mother learned from my grandmother, I have learned from my mother.

"My great-grandmother's education in the art of casting spells was cut short when most of her family and tribe were forced to move from the Mississippi area to Oklahoma. She and other family members did not make the trip. Instead they traveled northeast to the western areas of North Carolina and assimilated with the Cherokee. Once an adult, Mother moved further east and settled down with the Lumbee tribe of North Carolina. In my early twenties, I traveled further east to this area where I am today. Having never to take a husband, I have no children; thereby, the wisdom of the ages shall die with me."

Not wanting to insult her with a question about writing down her knowledge, I asked another question, "What do you remember about casting spells that could help me make sense of the hand incident?"

Her entire face lit up with the question; her posture changed, the strength of her voice became stronger, more precise as she became the teacher, and I became the student.

"Preparation is key when using a spell where demons are involved. You must always bind the demon first. If you cannot bind the demon, then the spell is too strong for you, and you should not proceed. Demons are vile and malicious and deceptive," she chuckled, "in that they can act like they are bound when in fact they are not. Spells with demons are the most dangerous and tricky!

"Very old spells did not include the knowledge about binding the demon, which means a powerful demon could knock you across a yard. In your story, the demon overpowered the men.

"Everyone with a soul is born with and protected by counter-curses bonds. If you think about it, a parent cannot put a harmful curse on a child. A guideline to help you understand bonds is that a parent–child bond is stronger than a sibling bond. A sibling bond is stronger than a friendship bond. A friendship bond is stronger than an acquaintance bond. For example, if a demon takes your soul or forces it from the body, counter-curse bond protection is lost forever. So very good, close, dear friends could get some protection from a demon, where an acquaintance bond is too weak to provide any protection from a demon.

"The strength of a spell is not the same at all times. A spell executed in a crescent lunar cycle is easier to counter than the same spell executed in a waxing lunar cycle. Knowing the moon phases: crescent, gibbous, waxing, and waning, it becomes easier to learn combination spells in waning gibbous, waning crescent, and others.

"After the first blue moon, all hope of breaking a spell is gone!

"Most of the strongest spells can be undone except if it is made to be unbreakable. These are the most dangerous and require the most preparation. Spells weaken over time unless it is made unbreakable.

"A spell is neither good nor bad, it is one of true desire or true intent.

"Spells have and need time agents, and the spell is in effect during that time. A good time agent is an old item that has been buried a long time preferably buried bones.

"Your story is one of naive men that found a very old spell and willed it like a toy, then before knowing what had happened, they had lost their souls to a demon that moved between them and killed them.

"Once freed, the demon moved into the man chanting the incantation. When the man realized what was happening to him, he then tried to quickly perform the role that usually is done by a third person—execute the counter-curse. *If there were only two men, then they had no chance of holding off the demon.* However, the man must have had a strong spiritual background because he was able to resist some of the demon's request. The first act of the demon would have been to try and stop him from initiating the counter-curse. But your story did not mention anything about a man picking up hot coals and shoving them into his mouth, gouging out his own eyes with sticks, or anything along that sort. Which leads me to conclude the one doing the incantation was a spiritual man. A third man would have served as the counter-curse. A third man would have spoken a truth of each man including himself, turned his back upon the other two. While facing away and ignoring the incantation, the demon would have been easier to manage. At no point in time, could the spell have been withdrawn or an untruth been spoken, especially during the first few minutes of a planting moon. At any time, if the third person withdraws a truth, he would have fatally wounded the demon, but at the same time, he would have lost his power forever. Which means his words would never come true again, he would never be able to participate in a spell even to protect himself. A third person has to be strong and able to endure pain because they can never go back on their words—a spiritual man would be ideal to exact a counter-curse.

"The type of curse described in the story requires earth and water, with water being the medium to transfer the curse. One of two things happened that night: (1) the men repeatedly transferred water from the creek to pour on the ground to keep the ground wet during the incantation or (2) the men submerged themselves into the creek, returned to the campsite soaking wet to complete the incantation, even then the ground would have to remain wet which leads me to think there had to be a third man.

"The demon moved into the second man by way of the wet earth they shared, then the demon quickly moved to attack the first man with a knife, and then a hatchet was used to cut off his hand.

"The demon then tortured the second man to maximize the pain on his body, probably by stabbing himself multiple times in the neck, chest, or stomach, and then the demon tried to suggest lying down into the warm comfortable fire, but the man was barely strong enough to fight off that suggestion and died with his hand over the fire. Once the host body died, the demon had only a few minutes to transfer into another host. Since all animals had fled the area and the ground was quickly drying, as a temporary measure, the demon entered into the severed hand. The moment of transference during a waxing gibbous moon had passed. The demon could sense that the only chance remaining for it to enter into another host was to get the blood from the severed arm to be converted into sacrificial smoke that the wind could then easily move throughout the woods until the essence of the demon could enter into another host: an animal, beast, or human.

"The campground security that night witnessed the panicking demon trying to position the arm over the fire, to squirt the last life of the man into the fire. After each squirt of blood into the fire, the hand jumped into the fire in hopes of being released into the smoke. The hand repeatedly left the fire, trying to move the body more in order to trick the heart to pump more blood into the fire. The demon was trapped with a botched unbreakable curse.

"Your story mentioned the temperament of the men changed from laughter to violence along with the mood of the woods. This is a classic move for a demon—the more pain it inflicts, the more cheerful it becomes, especially as the acts of violence increases, so does the laughter.

"The men had to have known the curse required three people at a minimum to execute it, four would have been better for more controlled results. If there was a third person, they had to have been shielded behind a waterfall, covered in snow, on the other side of a river or a body of water because the story mentioned only two men inside the campsite."

The lesson was over, I needed to leave. I found her answers to be very intuitive, and they gave me comfort. I thanked her for enlightening me on a possible sequence of events the night of the hand incident. I still had questions but not the time to wait for the answers. I helped the woman back to her house locked arm in arm.

Before I left, she grabbed my hand, then said, "The answer to your question, it's because I recognize the ancient curse of my ancestors."

For the next few months, I looked for every reason to return to the east coast, to return for a visit with the woman.

Six months later, in the wintertime, I had an opportunity to visit briefly again. She appeared to be frailer than when I saw her last.

I grabbed her hand and said hi. She said, “You are back already, Mr. Simpson!”

“How do you know it is me?”

She replied, “When you got out of the car, I could smell the cologne you put on this morning.”

“Wow, that is impressive, how are you feeling today?” I asked.

She replied, “Like a tired, old, dying woman.”

She smiled, and I smiled and said, “I am sure you will be with us another hundred years.”

“I sure hope not,” she quickly replied.

“I was in the area and wanted to pay you a visit.”

She patted my hand, smiled, and then replied, “And to ask how long a spell could last.” She continued to say, “The last time we talked, I quickly mentioned that spells are in effect for a period of time.

“Buried objects govern the duration of a spell, the object used in the spell was wrong because your story did not mention anyone dying immediately after touching a cursed object. *Remember, with each passing year, the onset of death is delayed an hour.* The object used was probably from an animal, a child younger than twelve, a woman, or a spiritual person. The duration of the spell is for twice the time the object had been buried. For the duration of the spell, the object becomes cursed and aligned with the bound demon. The best object to use in a spell is bone, however, the duration of a spell involving a demon must be set with bones of an evil person or person of ill repute.

"Powerful spells are usually done at the inundation of a full moon. In your story, the men executed the spell a week before a planting moon, which is a weaker spell.

"The strength of the spell upon the hand is unknown because the spell was not executed correctly, never completed, and initiated during a weaker lunar cycle. If there was a third man, he would definitely know the strength."

I asked, "Is there anything that can be done to destroy the hand or at least keep it from harming children?"

Her reply was one of hope, "There are thousands of people with strong counter-curse bonds because family bonds are stronger than acquaintance bonds. But to find knowledgeable people strong enough to execute the counter-curse is difficult and very stressful on the body, and I am too weak." She continued to say, "It is easy to talk about reversing the curse upon the hand, however, if you had the people for the counter-curse, how would you capture the hand?"

I told her the truth, "I have no idea!"

She smiled and said, "That is the easy part."

"How?" I asked quickly. I begged, "Please tell me."

Instead of answering the question, she asked, "What treats were left in the trees?"

I asked, "What do you mean?"

The woman said, "One way to make a curse unbreakable is to create splinters of the curse. All this means is to attach the curse to food that is left out in trees or on tree stumps for animals to eat and carry away. The further away the animal travels, the more difficult it is to collect the cursed splinters to undo a spell. This technique helps to make sure the splinters never find their way back. Usually, the animal dies and are often eaten by other animals, thereby creating more splinters of the curse. All the splinters would need to be retrieved and destroyed as a whole before starting to initiate the counter-curse."

She added, "I am just about certain the curse upon the hand has not been made unbreakable."

There was quiet around the campfire. More wood had been added to the fire. All eyes were on Keef and myself. Not knowing how to react, all waited for the next word to be spoken. The silence was finally broken when Keef asked, "What can be done about the hand?"

I replied, "Continue to follow the precautions you guys put in place, they seem to work."

Not satisfied with the answer, Keef asked, "Did the woman tell you how to trap the hand?"

I met with her one final time mid spring the following year. Her health had declined greatly; however, her face brightened upon my arrival. She held my hand as we talked at length about all things that interested her; she told me a lot about the life and times of her great-grandmother, grandmother, and mother as it was told to her. She asked if I had made any progress on the open questions surrounding the hand but did not offer much more insight into the hand incident. When I asked, "How can the hand be trapped?" she smiled and asked, "We are friends, aren't we?"

I replied, "Yes, Mama, we are."

She said, "You have the knowledge, I told you the counter-curse the first time we talked along the shore. I told you the vessel to be used the last time we talked." She smiled even wider and weakly squeezed my hand and said, "You will figure it out when the time comes." The smile on her face made her look years younger. I visited another hour, with plans of getting more answers in my next planned visit in six months. Two months later, I heard that she had passed away quietly the first night of a new moon in July.

A question was asked from the edge of the campsite, "What was the woman's name?"

"She said that her grandmother named her Chimalma, but her friends only knew her as Ms. Kaye or Ms. Henderson."

Next question was "What does her name mean?"

I replied, "I do not remember. You will need to visit a library and look it up."

Question, "Where was she from?"

Reply, "Her great-grandmother's name was Chicomecoatl, said that for generations her tribe had to travel north to escape foreign conquerors and that her tribe had been settled in the area east of the Mississippi delta for many years when they were forced to leave again."

Campers leaving the movie were now passing by, questions continued, "Where is the hand now?"

Keef replied, "I no longer work here and do not know! Ask the campground security the next time they drive through your area."

The people who had stopped to listen have started to leave. Some questions continued, "Mr. Simpson, have you figured out how to trap the hand?"

I replied, "No, not all of it. I am certain there are four things that are needed, I think I know one of the four."

A teenager asked, "What four things? I counted the woman gave only three to trap the hand."

Reply, "First, you have to lure the hand to the area of the incantation; second, keep it from leaving the area with a counter-curse; third, have three or four strong healthy men inside the protected area with the hand, one or more needs to be spiritual; and fourth, start the counter-spell to the incantation during a full moon."

Mark said, "I thought the first thing you would have to do is collect the splinters and destroy them."

I said, "That would be true if they existed, however, I do not think the curse was made unbreakable. So we don't need to collect the splinters because none exists."

Reena said, "I am not so sure because the food was cursed and then set out before the incantation was started."

Naya asked, "What would happen if you are wrong?"

Doubt and uncertainty crept back into my mind, and I said, "I do not know and do not want to find out."

Keef said, "Tonight has been very helpful for me. Now I have more information to help make sense of the hand incident."

I asked, "Is there any way that you can get more information around the investigation especially for the other side of the creek?"

Keef promised to look into the night of the hand incident with a new perspective. He would give extra attention to reports about the other side of the creek. He got up from his chair and said, "Thanks for the dinner, I need to be going." We exchanged phone numbers while the boys put their folding chairs back on the front seat of Keef's truck. Keef told them to get more wood off the back. The back lights of the truck shrank away into the night.

Around the campfire, fresh ideas flowed with how to trap and destroy the hand forever. Mr. Thompson's family returned to a very cold dinner.

Late into the night, whispers about the hand continued around the fire, pausing occasionally to listen whenever a new sound was heard in the distance. Too afraid to investigate, the campers added more wood to the fire. With wide eyes, the question was asked, "Mr. Simpson, does the campground scare you?"

"No, I enjoy the campground, however, some nights while in my tent, it feels like the hand is near, even near enough to hear something being dragged across leaves.

"If you know what to listen for, you too can hear the approach of the hand or the struggle of some unsuspecting animal trying to fight it off.

"Try it tonight, while in your sleeping bags, quietly listen, you may be able to hear the hand off in the distance. Do not move. Listen intently. The soft, scratchy sounds of the hand's movements are faint, whether it is far away or just about to pounce."

After cleaning up the food tent, I ushered the remaining campers off to bed before extinguishing the fire to mark the end of another day. I quickly prayed for all campers and then slept soundly until daybreak.

Printed in the United States
By Bookmasters